A Note to Parents and Caregivers:

Read-it! Readers are for children who are just starting on the amazing road to reading. These beautiful books support both the acquisition of reading skills and the love of books.

The RED LEVEL presents familiar topics using common words and repeating sentence patterns.
The BLUE LEVEL presents new ideas using a larger vocabulary and varied sentence structure.
The YELLOW LEVEL presents more challenging ideas, a broad vocabulary, and wide variety in sentence structure.

When sharing a book with your child, read in short stretches, pausing often to talk about the pictures. Have your child turn the pages and point to the pictures and familiar words. And be sure to reread favorite stories or parts of stories.

There is no right or wrong way to share books with children. Find time to read with your child, and pass on the legacy of literacy.

Adria F. Klein, Ph.D.
Professor Emeritus
California State University
San Bernardino, California

First American edition published in 2003 by
Picture Window Books
5115 Excelsior Boulevard
Suite 232
Minneapolis, MN 55416
1-877-845-8392
www.picturewindowbooks.com

First published in Great Britain by Franklin Watts, 96 Leonard Street, London, EC2A 4XD
Text © Penny Dolan 2000
Illustration © Deborah Allwright 2000

Printed in the United States of America.

Library of Congress Cataloging-in-Publication Data
Dolan, Penny.
  Mary and the fairy / written by Penny Dolan ; illustrated by Deborah Allwright.
    p. cm. — (Read-it! readers)
  Summary: Mary is sad because she has nothing to wear to the party, but the fairy who
arrives on the scene and tries to help doesn't quite understand the problem.
  ISBN 1-4048-0066-2
  [1. Fairies—Fiction. 2. Clothing and dress—Fiction. 3. Parties—Fiction.] I. Allwright,
Deborah, ill. II. Title. III. Series.
  PZ7.D6978 Mar 2003
  [E]—dc21
                                                          2002074802

PICTURE WINDOW BOOKS
Minneapolis, Minnesota

Mary and the Fairy

Written by Penny Dolan

Illustrated by Deborah Allwright

Reading Advisors:
Adria F. Klein, Ph.D.
Professor Emeritus, California State University
San Bernardino, California

Ruth Thomas
Durham Public Schools
Durham, North Carolina

R. Ernice Bookout
Durham Public Schools
Durham, North Carolina

Picture Window Books
Minneapolis, Minnesota

A fairy flew in through
Mary's window.

"Mary, why are you so sad?" she asked.

6

"I've got nothing to wear to the party," Mary said.

"Wait . . . " stammered Mary.

But the fairy wasn't
listening at all.

"How about a red gown?"
asked the fairy.

The red gown made
Mary feel very hot.
"But . . . " she said.

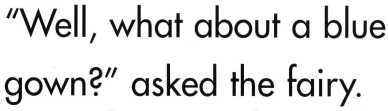

"Well, what about a blue gown?" asked the fairy.

The blue gown made
Mary feel very sad.
"No!" she said.

"I know! A yellow gown!" the fairy cried.

The yellow gown made
Mary's eyes very wiggly.

"I've got it this time! A green gown!" shouted the fairy.

The green gown made Mary's
tummy feel very wobbly.
"Yuck!" she said.

"No, don't tell me . . . you want a white gown!" guessed the fairy.

The white gown made
Mary feel very shivery.
"Stop!" shouted Mary.

"What color gown *do* you want?" asked the fairy angrily.

"I haven't got all day,
you know!"

"I don't want a gown," Mary sighed.

"What I really want is . . ."
Mary whispered to the fairy.

"Oh, I see!" said the fairy.

She waved her wand again.

"Is that right?" she asked.

"Oh, yes! Thank you, fairy," cried Mary.

"This is the perfect costume for the party."

Red Level

The Best Snowman, by Margaret Nash 1-4048-0048-4
Bill's Baggy Pants, by Susan Gates 1-4048-0050-6
Cleo and Leo, by Anne Cassidy 1-4048-0049-2
Felix on the Move, by Maeve Friel 1-4048-0055-7
Jasper and Jess, by Anne Cassidy 1-4048-0061-1
The Lazy Scarecrow, by Jillian Powell 1-4048-0062-X
Little Joe's Big Race, by Andy Blackford 1-4048-0063-8
The Little Star, by Deborah Nash 1-4048-0065-4
The Naughty Puppy, by Jillian Powell 1-4048-0067-0
Selfish Sophie, by Damian Kelleher 1-4048-0069-7

Blue Level

The Bossy Rooster, by Margaret Nash 1-4048-0051-4
Jack's Party, by Ann Bryant 1-4048-0060-3
Little Red Riding Hood, by Maggie Moore 1-4048-0064-6
Recycled!, by Jillian Powell 1-4048-0068-9
The Sassy Monkey, by Anne Cassidy 1-4048-0058-1
The Three Little Pigs, by Maggie Moore 1-4048-0071-9

Yellow Level

Cinderella, by Barrie Wade 1-4048-0052-2
The Crying Princess, by Anne Cassidy 1-4048-0053-0
Eight Enormous Elephants, by Penny Dolan 1-4048-0054-9
Freddie's Fears, by Hilary Robinson 1-4048-0056-5
Goldilocks and the Three Bears, by Barrie Wade 1-4048-0057-3
Mary and the Fairy, by Penny Dolan 1-4048-0066-2
Jack and the Beanstalk, by Maggie Moore 1-4048-0059-X
The Three Billy Goats Gruff, by Barrie Wade 1-4048-0070-0